Full Moon
Barnyard Dance

To Waldo, my full moon partner.
And to the Reed and Tacquard clans, whose mix is fun
enough for many a barnyard dance.
C. L. S.

Full Moon Barnyard Dance

CAROLE LEXA SCHAEFER

illustrated by

CHRISTINE DAVENIER

CANDLEWICK PRESS
CAMBRIDGE, MASSACHUSETTS

Once, on a night with a bright full moon,
the barnyard animals just could *not* settle down.
With twitchy ears they listened to the
crickets' sweet night tunes, *zweet-zweet-zweet* . . .

and to Frog's deep bass music,
thrum, thrum, thrum.

"What a moo-oon," crooned
the cow beside the barn.

"Maa-agnificent night,"
bleated a goat in the grass.

"Good for a snufflin' big dance,"
snorted a pig in the mud.

"Down by the pond," clucked
the hens from their nests.

"Right nee-ow," sang the cats   on the porch. "Nee-oww."

Two by two, the animals left the barnyard.

Cow and bull ambled. Goats pranced.
Pigs trotted. Roosters and hens scurried.
And the cats—they sashayed all the way to the pond.

There, by the light of the bright round moon,
cow and bull danced triple-step dips.

Goats together
billy-bobbed the bebop.

Pig pairs wibbled their very own jigs.

Hens and roosters flapped
a fancy fandango.

And the cats—they
slink-slanked the samba.

From the south—*reeoosh!*—
a rowdy wind blew in a crowd
of bumptious clouds.
They shut the moonlight out.
In the deep deep dark, the crickets,
zweet-zweet-zweet, and Frog,
thrum, thrum, thrum, sang on.

So, with a shrug, and a twirl,
and a swing, swirl, swing,
the barnyard animals kept dancing.

In the dark dark night, the bull murmured to the cow,
"My dear, did you say 'moo' or 'meow'?"

A rooster whispered,
"Hen, honey, your beak feels
soft as Piggy's snout."

The stoutest pig squealed, "Why, Mr. Hog, tonight
you're dancin' frisky as a kid!"

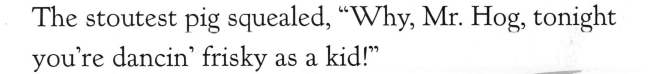

From the north—*shareesh!*—a swift wind
whisked the bumptious clouds away.
The animals danced in
moonlight again.

But when, two by two, they looked at each other — oh my, what a mix-up! What a tangle! What a muddle!

"You are not my partner," each one cried.

From the middle of the pond came
a deep *thrum, thrum.* Frog in his big voice
sang, "Twirl, swirl again—don't stop so soon.
Do some *new* partner dancing, by the light of the moon."

And—step, stomp, shuffle, twirl, swing, swirl—
that is just what the barnyard animals did, until . . .

they yawned and stretched and, two by two,
headed home to settle down at last.

"Huh," grunted the sleepy bull. "Tonight I danced the samba with a cat. Sort of nice."

"Mmph," mumbled a tired hen. "I jiggedy-jogged with a hog. Kind of friendly."

"Mighty neighborly," snuffled the stoutest pig, "me, billy-bobbing with a kid."

Down by the pond, a cricket chirped.
"Do you think such a dance will ever
happen again?"

"Uhm-hmm. It'll keep comin' round,"
thrummed Frog. He winked at the setting moon.
"'Cause everyone, mm-hmm, had fun."

First edition 2003

Library of Congress Cataloging-in-Publication Data

Schaefer, Carole Lexa.
Full moon barnyard dance / Carole Lexa Schaefer ;
illustrated by Christine Davenier.
p.   cm.
Summary: A beautiful night and a full moon inspire the barnyard animals
to hold a dance by the pond, where the arrival of some clouds provides
them with an unexpected experience.
ISBN 0-7636-1878-0
[1. Domestic animals—Fiction. 2. Dance—Fiction. 3. Moon—Fiction.]
I. Davenier, Christine, ill. II. Title.
PZ7.S3315 Fu 2003
[E]—dc21   2002023748

2 4 6 8 10 9 7 5 3 1

Printed in China

This book was typeset in Kennerley.
The illustrations were done in watercolor and ink.

Candlewick Press
2067 Massachusetts Avenue
Cambridge, Massachusetts 02140

visit us at www.candlewick.com